THE AGAMEMNON
OF
AESCHYLUS

by the same author

★

POEMS

THE AGAMEMNON
OF
AESCHYLUS

translated by
Louis MacNeice

Faber and Faber Limited
3 Queen Square
London

First published in 1936
by Faber and Faber Limited
3 Queen Square London W.C.1
First published in this edition 1967
Reprinted 1972
Printed in Great Britain by
John Dickens & Co Ltd
Northampton
All rights reserved

ISBN 0 571 08504 0

To
MY FATHER

PREFACE

(i) THE FAMILY TREE

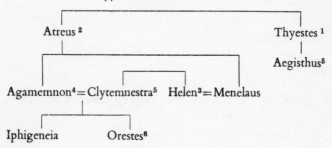

(ii) THE CHAIN OF CRIMES

Two brothers, Agamemnon and Menelaus, were kings of Argos. They married two sisters, Clytemnestra and Helen; each married to his cost. On the Greek view Helen and Clytemnestra were not just bad women; they were agents rather than creators of evil. Nobody on this view is either simply a protagonist of evil or simply a victim of circumstance. The family is physically, and therefore morally, a unit: the same blood runs in all, and through it descends an inherited responsibility which limits, without wholly destroying, the power of choice in each. The sins of the fathers are visited on the children, so the children are victims of circumstance. But the children, because they are of the same blood, are tempted to sin in their turn. If a man holds such a view he will tend

7

simultaneously to vindicate the ways of God and kick against the pricks of chance. It is this paradox that gives tension to a play like the Agamemnon. Here we have a chain of crimes, one leading on to another from generation to generation by a logic immanent in the blood and working through it. But the cause of the crimes, not only of the first link, the first crime, but present in every one of them, is the principle of Evil which logic cannot comprehend.

The chain of crimes in this play is as follows (see Family Tree above):

Past.

(1) Thyestes seduced Atreus' wife.
(2) Atreus killed Thyestes' young children and gave him them as meat.
(3) Helen forsook her husband and went to Troy with Paris.
(4) Agamemnon, to promote the Trojan War, sacrificed his daughter Iphigeneia.

Present.

(5) Aegisthus and Clytemnestra murder Agamemnon.

Future.

(6) Orestes will kill Aegisthus and his mother Clytemnestra.

(iii)

I have written this translation primarily for the stage. I have consciously sacrificed certain things in the original —notably the liturgical flavour of the diction and the metrical complexity of the choruses. It is my hope that the play emerges as a play and not as a museum piece.

My thanks are very much due to my friend, Professor E. R. Dodds, who, with a tolerance rare among scholars and a sympathy rare in anyone, read through the whole of my unacademic version and pointed out to me its more culpable inadequacies. The translation of certain passages is our joint product; but for the faults which remain I alone am responsible.

L. M.

1 *August* 1936

CHARACTERS

in order of their appearance

Watchman
Chorus of Old Men of the City
Clytemnestra
Herald
Agamemnon
Cassandra
Aegisthus

THE AGAMEMNON.

*(Scene. A space in front of the palace of Agamem-
non in Argos. Night. A* WATCHMAN *on
the roof of the palace.)*

WATCHMAN.

The gods it is I ask to release me from this watch
A year's length now, spending my nights like a dog,
Watching on my elbow on the roof of the sons of
 Atreus
So that I have come to know the assembly of the
 nightly stars
Those which bring storm and those which bring
 summer to men,
The shining Masters riveted in the sky—
I know the decline and rising of those stars.
And now I am waiting for the sign of the beacon,
The flame of fire that will carry the report from
 Troy,
News of her taking. Which task has been assigned me
By a woman of sanguine heart but a man's mind.
Yet when I take my restless rest in the soaking dew,
My night not visited with dreams—
For fear stands by me in the place of sleep
That I cannot firmly close my eyes in sleep—
Whenever I think to sing or hum to myself
As an antidote to sleep, then every time I groan
And fall to weeping for the fortunes of this house

Where not as before are things well ordered now.
But now may a good chance fall, escape from pain,
The good news visible in the midnight fire.

    (*Pause. A light appears, gradually increasing, the
       light of the beacon.*)

Ha! I salute you, torch of the night whose light
Is like the day, an earnest of many dances
In the city of Argos, celebration of Peace.
I call to Agamemnon's wife; quickly to rise
Out of her bed and in the house to raise
Clamour of joy in answer to this torch
For the city of Troy is taken—
Such is the evident message of the beckoning flame.
And I myself will dance my solo first
For I shall count my master's fortune mine
Now that this beacon has thrown me a lucky throw.
And may it be when he comes, the master of this
    house,
That I grasp his hand in my hand.
As to the rest, I am silent. A great ox, as they say,
Stands on my tongue. The house itself, if it took
    voice,
Could tell the case most clearly. But I will only
    speak
To those who know. For the others I remember
    nothing.

    (*Enter* CHORUS OF OLD MEN. *During the
       following chorus the day begins to dawn.*)

CHORUS. The tenth year it is since Priam's high
    Adversary, Menelaus the king
    And Agamemnon, the double-throned and sceptred
    Yoke of the sons of Atreus

Ruling in fee from God,
From this land gathered an Argive army
On a mission of war a thousand ships,
Their hearts howling in boundless bloodlust
In eagles' fashion who in lonely
Grief for nestlings above their homes hang
Turning in cycles
Beating the air with the oars of their wings,
   Now to no purpose
   Their love and task of attention.

But above there is One,
Maybe Pan, maybe Zeus or Apollo,
Who hears the harsh cries of the birds
Guests in his kingdom,
Wherefore, though late, in requital
He sends the Avenger.
Thus Zeus our master
Guardian of guest and of host
Sent against Paris the sons of Atreus
For a woman of many men
Many the dog-tired wrestlings
Limbs and knees in the dust pressed—
   For both the Greeks and Trojans
   An overture of breaking spears.

Things are where they are, will finish
In the manner fated and neither
Fire beneath nor oil above can soothe
The stubborn anger of the unburnt offering.
As for us, our bodies are bankrupt,
The expedition left us behind
And we wait supporting on sticks

Our strength—the strength of a child;
For the marrow that leaps in a boy's body
Is no better than that of the old
For the War God is not in his body
While the man who is very old
And his leaf withering away
Goes on the three-foot way
No better than a boy, and wanders
A dream in the middle of the day.

But you, daughter of Tyndareus,
Queen Clytemnestra,
What is the news, what is the truth, what have you.
    learnt,
On the strength of whose word have you thus
Sent orders for sacrifice round?
All the gods, the gods of the town,
Of the worlds of Below and Above,
By the door, in the square,
Have their altars ablaze with your gifts,
From here, from there, all sides, all corners.
Sky-high leap the flame-jets fed
By gentle and undeceiving
Persuasion of sacred unguent,
Oil from the royal stores.
Of these things tell
That which you can, that which you may,
Be healer of this our trouble
Which at times torments with evil
Though at times by propitiations
A shining hope repels
The insatiable thought upon grief
Which is eating away our hearts.

Of the omen which powerfully speeded
That voyage of strong men, by God's grace even I
Can tell, my age can still
Be galvanized to breathe the strength of song,
To tell how the kings of all the youth of Greece
Two-throned but one in mind
Were launched with pike and punitive hand
Against the Trojan shore by angry birds.
Kings of the birds to our kings came,
One with a white rump, the other black,
Appearing near the palace on the spear-arm side
Where all could see them,
Tearing a pregnant hare with the unborn young
Foiled of their courses.
    Cry, cry upon Death; but may the good prevail.

But the diligent prophet of the army seeing the sons
Of Atreus twin in temper knew
That the hare-killing birds were the two
Generals, explained it thus—
'In time this expedition sacks the town
Of Troy before whose towers
By Fate's force the public
Wealth will be wasted.
Only let not some spite from the gods benight the
    bulky battalions,
The bridle of Troy, nor strike them untimely;
For the goddess feels pity, is angry
With the winged dogs of her father
Who killed the cowering hare with her unborn
    young;
Artemis hates the eagles' feast.'
    Cry, cry upon Death; but may the good prevail.

'But though you are so kind, goddess,
To the little cubs of lions
And to all the sucking young of roving beasts
In whom your heart delights,
Fulfil us the signs of these things,
The signs which are good but open to blame,
And I call on Apollo the Healer
That his sister raise not against the Greeks
Unremitting gales to baulk their ships,
Hurrying on another kind of sacrifice, with no
     feasting,
Barbarous building of hates and disloyalties
Grown on the family. For anger grimly returns
Cunningly haunting the house, avenging the death
     of a child, never forgetting its due.'
So cried the prophet—evil and good together,
Fate that the birds foretold to the king's house.
In tune with this
   Cry, cry upon Death; but may the good prevail.

Zeus, whoever He is, if this
Be a name acceptable,
By this name I will call him.
There is no one comparable
When I reckon all of the case
Excepting Zeus, if ever I am to jettison
The barren care which clogs my heart.

Not He who formerly was great[1]
With brawling pride and mad for broils
Will even be said to have been.
And He who was next has met[2]

[1] Ouranos.   [2] Cronos.

18

His match and is seen no more,
But Zeus is the name to cry in your triumph-song
And win the prize for wisdom.

Who setting us on the road
Made this a valid law—
   'That men must learn by suffering.'
Drop by drop in sleep upon the heart
Falls the laborious memory of pain,
Against one's will comes wisdom;
The grace of the gods is forced on us
   Throned inviolably.

So at that time the elder
Chief of the Greek ships
Would not blame any prophet
Nor face the flail of fortune;
For unable to sail, the people
Of Greece were heavy with famine,
Waiting in Aulis where the tides
   Flow back, opposite Chalcis.

But the winds that blew from the Strymon,
Bringing delay, hunger, evil harbourage,
Crazing men, rotting ships and cables,
By drawing out the time
Were shredding into nothing the flower of Argos,
When the prophet screamed a new
Cure for that bitter tempest
And heavier still for the chiefs,
Pleading the anger of Artemis so that the sons of
    Atreus
Beat the ground with their sceptres and shed tears.

Then the elder king found voice and answered:
'Heavy is my fate, not obeying,
And heavy it is if I kill my child, the delight of my
      house,
And with a virgin's blood upon the altar
Make foul her father's hands.
Either alternative is evil.
How can I betray the fleet
And fail the allied army?
It is right they should passionately cry for the winds
      to be lulled
By the blood of a girl. So be it. May it be well.'

But when he had put on the halter of Necessity
Breathing in his heart a veering wind of evil
Unsanctioned, unholy, from that moment forward
He changed his counsel, would stop at nothing.
For the heart of man is hardened by infatuation,
A faulty adviser, the first link of sorrow.
Whatever the cause, he brought himself to slay
His daughter, an offering to promote the voyage
To a war for a runaway wife.

Her prayers and her cries of father,
Her life of a maiden,
Counted for nothing with those militarists;
But her father, having duly prayed, told the attendants
To lift her, like a goat, above the altar
With her robes falling about her,
To lift her boldly, her spirit fainting,
And hold back with a gag upon her lovely mouth
By the dumb force of a bridle
The cry which would curse the house.

Then dropping on the ground her saffron dress,
Glancing at each of her appointed
Sacrificers a shaft of pity,
Plain as in a picture she wished
To speak to them by name, for often
At her father's table where men feasted
She had sung in celebration for her father
With a pure voice, affectionately, virginally,
The hymn for happiness at the third libation.
The sequel to this I saw not and tell not
But the crafts of Calchas gained their object.
To learn by suffering is the equation of Justice; the
     Future
Is known when it comes, let it go till then.
To know in advance is to sorrow in advance.
The facts will appear with the shining of the dawn.
              (*Enter* CLYTEMNESTRA.)
But may good, at the least, follow after
As the queen here wishes, who stands
Nearest the throne, the only
     Defence of the land of Argos.

LEADER OF THE CHORUS.

   I have come, Clytemnestra, reverencing your au-
      thority.
   For it is right to honour our master's wife
   When the man's own throne is empty.
   But you, if you have heard good news for certain,
      or if
   You sacrifice on the strength of flattering hopes,
   I would gladly hear. Though I cannot cavil at
      silence.

CLYTEMNESTRA.

   Bearing good news, as the proverb says, may Dawn

Spring from her mother Night.

You will hear something now that was beyond your hopes.

The men of Argos have taken Priam's city.

LEADER. What! I cannot believe it. It escapes me.

CLYT.

Troy in the hands of the Greeks. Do I speak plain?

LEADER. Joy creeps over me, calling out my tears.

CLYT. Yes. Your eyes proclaim your loyalty.

LEADER. But what are your grounds? Have you a proof of it?

CLYT. There is proof indeed—unless God has cheated us.

LEADER. Perhaps you believe the inveigling shapes of dreams?

CLYT. I would not be credited with a dozing brain!

LEADER. Or are you puffed up by Rumour, the wingless flyer?

CLYT. You mock my common sense as if I were a child.

LEADER. But at what time was the city given to sack?

CLYT. In this very night that gave birth to this day.

LEADER. What messenger could come so fast?

CLYT. Hephaestus, launching a fine flame from Ida,
Beacon forwarding beacon, despatch-riders of fire,
Ida relayed to Hermes' cliff in Lemnos
And the great glow from the island was taken over third
By the height of Athos that belongs to Zeus,
And towering then to straddle over the sea
The might of the running torch joyfully tossed
The gold gleam forward like another sun,
Herald of light to the heights of Mount Macistus,

And he without delay, nor carelessly by sleep
Encumbered, did not shirk his intermediary role,
His farflung ray reached the Euripus' tides
And told Messapion's watchers, who in turn
Sent on the message further
Setting a stack of dried-up heather on fire.
And the strapping flame, not yet enfeebled, leapt
Over the plain of Asopus like a blazing moon
And woke on the crags of Cithaeron
Another relay in the chain of fire.
The light that was sent from far was not declined
By the look-out men, who raised a fiercer yet,
A light which jumped the water of Gorgopis
And to Mount Aegiplanctus duly come
Urged the reveille of the punctual fire.
So then they kindle it squanderingly and launch
A beard of flame big enough to pass
The headland that looks down upon the Saronic
     gulf,
Blazing and bounding till it reached at length
The Arachnaean steep, our neighbouring heights;
And leaps in the latter end on the roof of the sons of
     Atreus
Issue and image of the fire on Ida.
Such was the assignment of my torch-racers,
The task of each fulfilled by his successor,
And victor is he who ran both first and last.
Such is the proof I offer you, the sign
My husband sent me out of Troy.

LEADER.

To the gods, queen, I shall give thanks presently.
But I would like to hear this story further,
To wonder at it in detail from your lips.

23

CLYT. The Greeks hold Troy upon this day.
　　　The cries in the town I fancy do not mingle.
　　　Pour oil and vinegar into the same jar,
　　　You would say they stand apart unlovingly;
　　　Of those who are captured and those who have
　　　　　conquered
　　　Distinct are the sounds of their diverse fortunes,
　　　For *these* having flung themselves about the bodies
　　　Of husbands and brothers, or sons upon the bodies
　　　Of aged fathers from a throat no longer
　　　Free, lament the fate of their most loved.
　　　But *those* a night's marauding after battle
　　　Sets hungry to what breakfast the town offers
　　　Not billeted duly in any barracks order
　　　But as each man has drawn his lot of luck.
　　　So in the captive homes of Troy already
　　　They take their lodging, free of the frosts
　　　And dews of the open. Like happy men
　　　They will sleep all night without sentry.
　　　But if they respect duly the city's gods,
　　　Those of the captured land and the sanctuaries of
　　　　　the gods,
　　　They need not, having conquered, fear reconquest.
　　　But let no lust fall first upon the troops
　　　To plunder what is not right, subdued by gain,
　　　For they must still, in order to come home safe,
　　　Get round the second lap of the doubled course.
　　　So if they return without offence to the gods
　　　The grievance of the slain may learn at last
　　　A friendly talk—unless some fresh wrong falls.
　　　Such are the thoughts you hear from me, a woman.
　　　But may the good prevail for all to see.
　　　We have much good. I only ask to enjoy it.

LEADER.
    Woman, you speak with sense like a prudent man.
    I, who have heard your valid proofs, prepare
    To give the glory to God.
    Fair recompense is brought us for our troubles.
            (CLYTEMNESTRA *goes back into the palace*.)
CHORUS. O Zeus our king and Night our friend
    Donor of glories,
    Night who cast on the towers of Troy
    A close-clinging net so that neither the grown
    Nor any of the children can pass
    The enslaving and huge
    Trap of all-taking destruction.
    Great Zeus, guardian of host and guest,
    I honour who has done his work and taken
    A leisured aim at Paris so that neither
    Too short nor yet over the stars
        He might shoot to no purpose.

    From Zeus is the blow they can tell of,
    This at least can be established,
    They have fared according to his ruling. For some
    Deny that the gods deign to consider those among
            men
    Who trample on the grace of inviolate things;
    It is the impious man says this,
    For Ruin is revealed the child
    Of not to be attempted actions
    When men are puffed up unduly
    And their houses are stuffed with riches.
    Measure is the best. Let danger be distant,
    This should suffice a man
    With a proper part of wisdom.

25

For a man has no protection
Against the drunkenness of riches
Once he has spurned from his sight
The high altar of Justice.

Sombre Persuasion compels him,
Intolerable child of calculating Doom;
All cure is vain, there is no glozing it over
But the mischief shines forth with a deadly light
And like bad coinage
By rubbings and frictions
He stands discoloured and black
Under the test—like a boy
Who chases a winged bird
He has branded his city for ever.
His prayers are heard by no god;
Who makes such things his practice
The gods destroy him.
    This way came Paris
    To the house of the sons of Atreus
    And outraged the table of friendship
    Stealing the wife of his host.

Leaving to her countrymen clanging of
Shields and of spears and
Launching of warships
And bringing instead of a dowry destruction to
    Troy
Lightly she was gone through the gates daring
Things undared. Many the groans
Of the palace spokesmen on this theme—
'O the house, the house, and its princes,
O the bed and the imprint of her limbs;

One can see him crouching in silence
Dishonoured and unreviling.'
Through desire for her who is overseas, a ghost
Will seem to rule the household.
    And now her husband hates
    The grace of shapely statues;
    In the emptiness of their eyes
    All their appeal is departed.

But appearing in dreams persuasive
Images come bringing a joy that is vain,
Vain for when in fancy he looks to touch her—
Slipping through his hands the vision
Rapidly is gone
Following on wings the walks of sleep.
Such are his griefs in his house on his hearth,
Such as these and worse than these,
But everywhere through the land of Greece which
    men have left
Are mourning women with enduring hearts
To be seen in all houses; many
Are the thoughts which stab their hearts;
    For those they sent to war
    They know, but in place of men
    That which comes home to them
    Is merely an urn and ashes.

But the money-changer War, changer of bodies,
Holding his balance in the battle
Home from Troy refined by fire
Sends back to friends the dust
That is heavy with tears, stowing
A man's worth of ashes

27

In an easily handled jar.
And they wail speaking well of the men how that
    one
Was expert in battle, and one fell well in the
    carnage—
But for another man's wife.
Muffled and muttered words;
And resentful grief creeps up against the sons
Of Atreus and their cause.
    But others there by the wall
    Entombed in Trojan ground
    Lie, handsome of limb,
    Holding and hidden in enemy soil.

Heavy is the murmur of an angry people
Performing the purpose of a public curse;
There is something cowled in the night
That I anxiously wait to hear.
For the gods are not blind to the
Murderers of many and the black
Furies in time
When a man prospers in sin
By erosion of life reduce him to darkness,
Who, once among the lost, can no more
Be helped. Over-great glory
Is a sore burden. The high peak
Is blasted by the eyes of Zeus.
    I prefer an unenvied fortune,
    Not to be a sacker of cities
    Nor to find myself living at another's
    Ruling, myself a captive.
AN OLD MAN. From the good news' beacon a swift
    Rumour is gone through the town.

Who knows if it be true
Or some deceit of the gods?

ANOTHER O.M. Who is so childish or broken in wit
To kindle his heart at a new-fangled message of
flame
And then be downcast
At a change of report?

ANOTHER O.M. It fits the temper of a woman
To give her assent to a story before it is proved.

ANOTHER O.M.
The over-credulous passion of women expands
In swift conflagration but swiftly declining is gone
The news that a woman announced.

LEADER OF THE CHORUS.
Soon we shall know about the illuminant torches,
The beacons and the fiery relays,
Whether they were true or whether like dreams
That pleasant light came here and hoaxed our wits.
Look: I see, coming from the beach, a herald
Shadowed with olive shoots; the dust upon him,
Mud's thirsty sister and colleague, is my witness
That he will not give dumb news nor news by
lighting
A flame of fire with the smoke of mountain timber;
In words he will either corroborate our joy—
But the opposite version I reject with horror.
To the good appeared so far may good be added.

ANOTHER SPEAKER.
Whoever makes other prayers for this our city,
May he reap himself the fruits of his wicked heart.
            (*Enter the* HERALD, *who kisses the ground before
            speaking.*)

HERALD. Earth of my fathers, O the earth of Argos,

In the light of the tenth year I reach you thus
After many shattered hopes achieving one,
For never did I dare to think that here in Argive land
I should win a grave in the dearest soil of home;
But now hail, land, and hail, light of the sun,
And Zeus high above the country and the Pythian
     king—
May he no longer shoot his arrows at us
(Implacable long enough beside Scamander)
But now be saviour to us and be healer,
King Apollo. And all the Assembly's gods
I call upon, and him my patron, Hermes,
The dear herald whom all heralds adore,
And the Heroes who sped our voyage, again with
     favour
Take back the army that has escaped the spear.
O cherished dwelling, palace of royalty,
O august thrones and gods facing the sun,
If ever before, now with your bright eyes
Gladly receive your king after much time,
Who comes bringing light to you in the night time,
And to all these as well—King Agamemnon.
Give him a good welcome as he deserves,
Who with the axe of judgment-awarding God
Has smashed Troy and levelled the Trojan land;
The altars are destroyed, the seats of the gods,
And the seed of all the land is perished from it.
Having cast this halter round the neck of Troy
The King, the elder son of Atreus, a blessed man,
Comes, the most worthy to have honour of all
Men that are now. Paris nor his guilty city
Can boast that the crime was greater than the atone-
     ment.

Convicted in a suit for rape and robbery
He has lost his stolen goods and with consummate ruin
Mowed down the whole country and his father's
house.
The sons of Priam have paid their account with
interest.

LEADER OF THE CHORUS.

Hail and be glad, herald of the Greek army.

HERALD.

Yes. Glad indeed! So glad that at the gods' demand
I should no longer hesitate to die.

LEADER. Were you so harrowed by desire for home?

HERALD. Yes. The tears come to my eyes for joy.

LEADER. Sweet then is the fever which afflicts you.

HERALD. What do you mean? Let me learn your drift.

LEADER. Longing for those whose love came back in
echo.

HERALD. Meaning the land was homesick for the army?

LEADER.

Yes. I would often groan from a darkened heart.

HERALD. This sullen hatred—how did it fasten on you?

LEADER. I cannot say. Silence is my stock prescription.

HERALD. What? In your masters' absence were there
some you feared?

LEADER. Yes. In your phrase, death would now be a
gratification.

HERALD. Yes, for success is ours. These things have taken
time.
Some of them we could say have fallen well,
While some we blame. Yet who except the gods
Is free from pain the whole duration of life?
If I were to tell of our labours, our hard lodging,
The sleeping on crowded decks, the scanty blankets,

31

Tossing and groaning, rations that never reached
      us—
And the land too gave matter for more disgust,
For our beds lay under the enemy's walls.
Continuous drizzle from the sky, dews from the
      marshes,
Rotting our clothes, filling our hair with lice.
And if one were to tell of the bird-destroying
      winter
Intolerable from the snows of Ida
Or of the heat when the sea slackens at noon
Waveless and dozing in a depressed calm—
But why make these complaints? The weariness is
      over;
Over indeed for some who never again
Need even trouble to rise.
Why make a computation of the lost?
Why need the living sorrow for the spites of
      fortune?
I wish to say a long goodbye to disasters.
For us, the remnant of the troops of Argos,
The advantage remains, the pain can not outweigh
      it;
So we can make our boast to this sun's light,
Flying on words above the land and sea:
'Having taken Troy the Argive expedition
Has nailed up throughout Greece in every temple
These spoils, these ancient trophies.'
Those who hear such things must praise the city
And the generals. And the grace of God be
      honoured
Which brought these things about. You have the
      whole story.

32

LEADER. I confess myself convinced by your report.
    Old men are always young enough to learn.
      (*Enter* CLYTEMNESTRA *from the palace.*)
    This news belongs by right first to the house
    And Clytemnestra—though I am enriched also.
CLYT. Long before this I shouted at joy's command
    At the coming of the first night-messenger of fire
    Announcing the taking and capsizing of Troy.
    And people reproached me saying, 'Do mere
      beacons
    Persuade you to think that Troy is already down?
    Indeed a woman's heart is easily exalted.'
    Such comments made me seem to be wandering
      but yet
    I began my sacrifices and in the women's fashion
    Throughout the town they raised triumphant cries
    And in the gods' enclosures
    Lulling the fragrant, incense-eating flame.
    And now what need is there for you to tell me
      more?
    From the King himself I shall learn the whole story.
    But how the best to welcome my honoured lord
    I shall take pains when he comes back—For what
    Is a kinder light for a woman to see than this,
    To open the gates to her man come back from war
    When God has saved him? Tell this to my husband,
    To come with all speed, the city's darling;
    May he returning find a wife as loyal
    As when he left her, watchdog of the house,
    Good to *him* but fierce to the ill-intentioned,
    And in all other things as ever, having destroyed
    No seal or pledge at all in the length of time.
    I know no pleasure with another man, no scandal,

More than I know how to dye metal red.
Such is my boast, bearing a load of truth,
A boast that need not disgrace a noble wife.

(Exit.)

LEADER. Thus has she spoken; if you take her meaning,
Only a specious tale to shrewd interpreters.
But do you, herald, tell me; I ask after Menelaus
Whether he will, returning safe preserved,
Come back with you, our land's loved master.

HERALD. I am not able to speak the lovely falsehood
To profit you, my friends, for any stretch of time.

LEADER. But if only the true tidings could be also good!
It is hard to hide a division of good and true.

HERALD. The prince is vanished out of the Greek fleet,
Himself and ship. I speak no lie.

LEADER.
Did he put forth first in the sight of all from Troy,
Or a storm that troubled all sweep him apart?

HERALD. You have hit the target like a master archer,
Told succinctly a long tale of sorrow.

LEADER.
Did the rumours current among the remaining ships
Represent him as alive or dead?

HERALD. No one knows so as to tell for sure
Except the sun who nurses the breeds of earth.

LEADER.
Tell me how the storm came on the host of ships
Through the divine anger, and how it ended.

HERALD.
Day of good news should not be fouled by tongue
That tells ill news. To each god his season.
When, despair in his face, a messenger brings to a
town

34

The hated news of a fallen army—
One general wound to the city and many men
Outcast, outcursed, from many homes
By the double whip which War is fond of,
Doom with a bloody spear in either hand,
One carrying such a pack of grief could well
Recite this hymn of the Furies at your asking.
But when our cause is saved and a messenger of
    good
Comes to a city glad with festivity,
How am I to mix good news with bad, recounting
The storm that meant God's anger on the Greeks?
For they swore together, those inveterate enemies,
Fire and sea, and proved their alliance, destroying
The unhappy troops of Argos.
In night arose ill-waved evil,
Ships on each other the blasts from Thrace
Crashed colliding, which butting with horns in the
    violence
Of big wind and rattle of rain were gone
To nothing, whirled all ways by a wicked shepherd.
But when there came up the shining light of the sun
We saw the Aegean sea flowering with corpses
Of Greek men and their ships' wreckage.
But for us, our ship was not damaged,
Whether someone snatched it away or begged it
    off,
Some god, not a man, handling the tiller;
And Saving Fortune was willing to sit upon our
    ship
So that neither at anchor we took the tilt of waves
Nor ran to splinters on the crag-bound coast.
But then having thus escaped death on the sea,

In the white day, not trusting our fortune,
We pastured this new trouble upon our thoughts,
The fleet being battered, the sailors weary,
And now if any of *them* still draw breath,
They are thinking no doubt of us as being lost
And we are thinking of them as being lost.
May the best happen. As for Menelaus
The first guess and most likely is a disaster.
But still—if any ray of sun detects him
Alive, with living eyes, by the plan of Zeus
Not yet resolved to annul the race completely,
There is some hope then that he will return home.
So much you have heard. Know that it is the truth.

(*Exit.*)

CHORUS. Who was it named her thus
    In all ways appositely
    Unless it was Someone whom we do not see,
    Fore-knowing fate
    And plying an accurate tongue?
    Helen, bride of spears and conflict's
    Focus, who as was befitting
    Proved a hell to ships and men,
    Hell to her country, sailing
    Away from delicately-sumptuous curtains,
    Away on the wind of a giant Zephyr,
    And shielded hunters mustered many
    On the vanished track of the oars,
    Oars beached on the leafy
    Banks of a Trojan river
    For the sake of bloody war.

    But on Troy was thrust a marring marriage
    By the Wrath that working to an end exacts

36

In time a price from guests
Who dishonoured their host
And dishonoured Zeus of the Hearth,
From those noisy celebrants
Of the wedding hymn which fell
To the brothers of Paris
To sing upon that day.
But learning this, unlearning that,
Priam's ancestral city now
Continually mourns, reviling
Paris the fatal bridegroom.
The city has had much sorrow,
Much desolation in life,
From the pitiful loss of her people.

So in his house a man might rear
A lion's cub caught from the dam
In need of suckling,
In the prelude of its life
Mild, gentle with children,
For old men a playmate,
Often held in the arms
Like a new-born child,
Wheedling the hand,
Fawning at belly's bidding.

But matured by time he showed
The temper of his stock and payed
Thanks for his fostering
With disaster of slaughter of sheep
Making an unbidden banquet
And now the house is a shambles,
Irremediable grief to its people,

Calamitous carnage:
For the pet they had fostered was sent
By God as a priest of Ruin.

So I would say there came
To the city of Troy
A notion of windless calm,
Delicate adornment of riches,
Soft shooting of the eyes and flower
Of desire that stings the fancy.
But swerving aside she achieved
A bitter end to her marriage,
Ill guest and ill companion,
Hurled upon Priam's sons, convoyed
By Zeus, patron of guest and host,
Dark angel dowered with tears.

Long current among men an old saying
Runs that a man's prosperity
When grown to greatness
Comes to the birth, does not die childless—
His good luck breeds for his house
Distress that shall not be appeased.
I only, apart from the others,
Hold that the unrighteous action
Breeds true to its kind,
Leaves its own children behind it.
But the lot of a righteous house
Is a fair offspring always.

Ancient self-glory is accustomed
To bear to light in the evil sort of men
A new self-glory and madness,

Which sometime or sometime finds
The appointed hour for its birth,
And born therewith is the Spirit, intractable, un-
    holy, irresistible,
The reckless lust that brings black Doom upon the
    house,
A child that is like its parents.

But Honest Dealing is clear
Shining in smoky homes,
Honours the god-fearing life.
Mansions gilded by filth of hands she leaves,
Turns her eyes elsewhere, visits the innocent house,
Not respecting the power
Of wealth mis-stamped with approval,
But guides all to the goal.

    (*Enter* AGAMEMNON *and* CASSANDRA *on chariots*.)

CHORUS. Come then my King, stormer of Troy,
    Offspring of Atreus,
    How shall I hail you, how give you honour
    Neither overshooting nor falling short
        Of the measure of homage?
    There are many who honour appearance too much
    Passing the bounds that are right.
    To condole with the unfortunate man
    Each one is ready but the bite of the grief
        Never goes through to the heart.
    And they join in rejoicing, affecting to share it,
    Forcing their face to a smile.
    But he who is shrewd to shepherd his sheep
    Will fail not to notice the eyes of a man
    Which seem to be loyal but lie,
        Fawning with watery friendship.

Even you, in my thought, when you marshalled the
   troops
For Helen's sake, I will not hide it,
Made a harsh and ugly picture,
Holding badly the tiller of reason,
Paying with the death of men
   Ransom for a willing whore.
But now, not unfriendly, not superficially,
I offer my service, well-doers' welcome.
In time you will learn by inquiry
Who has done rightly, who transgressed
   In the work of watching the city.

AGAMEMNON.

First to Argos and the country's gods
My fitting salutations, who have aided me
To return and in the justice which I exacted
From Priam's city. Hearing the unspoken case
The gods unanimously had cast their vote
Into the bloody urn for the massacre of Troy;
But to the opposite urn
Hope came, dangled her hand, but did no more.
Smoke marks even now the city's capture.
Whirlwinds of doom are alive, the dying ashes
Spread on the air the fat savour of wealth.
For these things we must pay some memorable
   return
To Heaven, having exacted enormous vengeance
For wife-rape; for a woman
The Argive monster ground a city to powder,
Sprung from a wooden horse, shield-wielding folk,
Launching a leap at the setting of the Pleiads,
Jumping the ramparts, a ravening lion,
Lapped its fill of the kingly blood.

To the gods I have drawn out this overture
But as for your concerns, I bear them in my mind
And say the same, you have me in agreement.
To few of men does it belong by nature
To congratulate their friends unenviously,
For a sullen poison fastens on the heart,
Doubling the pain of a man with this disease;
He feels the weight of his own griefs and when
He sees another's prosperity he groans.
I speak with knowledge, being well acquainted
With the mirror of comradeship—ghost of a
    shadow
Were those who seemed to be so loyal to me.
Only Odysseus, who sailed against his will,
Proved, when yoked with me, a ready tracehorse;
I speak of him not knowing if he is alive.
But for what concerns the city and the gods
Appointing public debates in full assembly
We shall consult. That which is well already
We shall take steps to ensure it remain well.
But where there is need of medical remedies,
By applying benevolent cautery or surgery
We shall try to deflect the dangers of disease.
But now, entering the halls where stands my hearth,
First I shall make salutation to the gods
Who sent me a far journey and have brought me
    back.
And may my victory not leave my side.
        (*Enter* CLYTEMNESTRA, *followed by women slaves
        carrying purple tapestries.*)
CLYT. Men of the city, you the aged of Argos,
    I shall feel no shame to describe to you my love
    Towards my husband. Shyness in all of us

Wears thin with time. Here are the facts first hand.
I will tell you of my own unbearable life
I led so long as this man was at Troy.
For first that the woman separate from her man
Should sit alone at home is extreme cruelty,
Hearing so many malignant rumours—First
Comes one, and another comes after, bad news to
  worse,
Clamour of grief to the house. If Agamemnon
Had had so many wounds as those reported
Which poured home through the pipes of hearsay,
  then—
Then he would be gashed fuller than a net has holes!
And if only he had died . . . as often as rumour told
  us,
He would be like the giant in the legend,
Three-bodied. Dying once for every body,
He should have by now three blankets of earth
  above him—
All that above him; I care not how deep the mat-
  tress under!
Such are the malignant rumours thanks to which
They have often seized me against my will and
  undone
The loop of a rope from my neck.
And this is why our son is not standing here,
The guarantee of your pledges and mine,
As he should be, Orestes. Do not wonder;
He is being brought up by a friendly ally and host,
Strophius the Phocian, who warned me in advance
Of dubious troubles, both your risks at Troy
And the anarchy of shouting mobs that might
Overturn policy, for it is born in men

To kick the man who is down.
This is not a disingenuous excuse.
For me the outrushing wells of weeping are dried
    up,
There is no drop left in them.
My eyes are sore from sitting late at nights
Weeping for you and for the baffled beacons,
Never lit up. And, when I slept, in dreams
I have been waked by the thin whizz of a buzzing
Gnat, seeing more horrors fasten on you
Than could take place in the mere time of my
    dream.
Having endured all this, now, with unsorrowed
    heart
I would hail this man as the watchdog of the farm,
Forestay that saves the ship, pillar that props
The lofty roof, appearance of an only son
To a father or of land to sailors past their hope,
The loveliest day to see after the storm,
Gush of well-water for the thirsty traveller.
Such are the metaphors I think befit him,
But envy be absent. Many misfortunes already
We have endured. But now, dear head, come
    down
Out of that car, not placing upon the ground
Your foot, O King, the foot that trampled Troy.
Why are you waiting, slaves, to whom the task is
    assigned
To spread the pavement of his path with tapestries?
At once, at once let his way be strewn with purple
That Justice lead him toward his unexpected home.
The rest a mind, not overcome by sleep
Will arrange rightly, with God's help, as destined.

AGAM. Daughter of Leda, guardian of my house,
    You have spoken in proportion to my absence.
    You have drawn your speech out long. Duly to
        praise me,
    That is a duty to be performed by others.
    And further—do not by women's methods make
        me
    Effeminate nor in barbarian fashion
    Gape ground-grovelling acclamations at me
    Nor strewing my path with cloths make it invidi-
        ous.
    It is the gods should be honoured in this way.
    But being mortal to tread embroidered beauty
    For me is no way without fear.
    I tell you to honour me as a man, not god.
    Footcloths are very well—Embroidered stuffs
    Are stuff for gossip. And not to think unwisely
    Is the greatest gift of God. Call happy only him
    Who has ended his life in sweet prosperity.
    I have spoken. This thing I could not do with con-
        fidence.
CLYT. Tell me now, according to your judgment.
AGAM. I tell you you shall not override my judgment.
CLYT. Supposing you had feared something . . .
    Could you have vowed to God to do this thing?
AGAM. Yes. If an expert had prescribed that vow.
CLYT. And how would Priam have acted in your place?
AGAM.
    He would have trod the cloths, I think, for certain.
CLYT. Then do not flinch before the blame of men.
AGAM. The voice of the multitude is very strong.
CLYT. But the man none envy is not enviable.
AGAM. It is not a woman's part to love disputing.

CLYT. But it is a conqueror's part to yield upon occasion.

AGAM. You think such victory worth fighting for?

CLYT. Give way. Consent to let me have the mastery.

AGAM. Well, if such is your wish, let someone quickly loose

My vassal sandals, underlings of my feet,

And stepping on these sea-purples may no god

Shoot me from far with the envy of his eye.

Great shame it is to ruin my house and spoil

The wealth of costly weavings with my feet.

But of this matter enough. This stranger woman here

Take in with kindness. The man who is a gentle master

God looks on from far off complacently.

For no one of his will bears the slave's yoke.

This woman, of many riches being the chosen

Flower, gift of the soldiers, has come with me.

But since I have been prevailed on by your words

I will go to my palace home, treading on purples.

   (*He dismounts from the chariot and begins to walk
         up the tapestried path. During the following
         speech he enters the palace.*)

CLYT. There is the sea and who shall drain it dry? It breeds

Its wealth in silver of plenty of purple gushing

And ever-renewed, the dyeings of our garments.

The house has its store of these by God's grace, King.

This house is ignorant of poverty

And I would have vowed a pavement of many garments

Had the palace oracle enjoined that vow

45

Thereby to contrive a ransom for his life.
For while there is root, foliage comes to the house
Spreading a tent of shade against the Dog Star.
So now that you have reached your hearth and
    home
You prove a miracle—advent of warmth in winter;
And further this—even in the time of heat
When God is fermenting wine from the bitter
    grape,
Even then it is cool in the house if only
Its master walk at home, a grown man, ripe.
O Zeus the Ripener, ripen these my prayers;
Your part it is to make the ripe fruit fall.

                  (She enters the palace.)

CHORUS. Why, why at the doors
    Of my fore-seeing heart
    Does this terror keep beating its wings?
    And my song play the prophet
    Unbidden, unhired—
    Which I cannot spit out
    Like the enigmas of dreams
    Nor plausible confidence
    Sit on the throne of my mind?
    It is long time since
    The cables let down from the stern
    Were chafed by the sand when the sea-
      faring army started for Troy.

    And I learn with my eyes
    And witness myself their return;
    But the hymn without lyre goes up,
    The dirge of the Avenging Fiend,
    In the depths of my self-taught heart

Which has lost its dear
Possession of the strength of hope.
But my guts and my heart
Are not idle which seethe with the waves
Of trouble nearing its hour.
But I pray that these thoughts
May fall out not as I think
　And not be fulfilled in the end.

Truly when health grows much
It respects not limit; for disease,
Its neighbour in the next door room,
Presses upon it.
A man's life, crowding sail,
Strikes on the blind reef:
But if caution in advance
Jettison part of the cargo
With the derrick of due proportion,
The whole house does not sink,
Though crammed with a weight of woe
The hull does not go under.
The abundant bounty of God
And his gifts from the year's furrows
Drive the famine back.

But when upon the ground there has fallen once
The black blood of a man's death,
Who shall summon it back by incantations?
Even Asclepius who had the art
To fetch the dead to life, even to him
Zeus put a provident end.
But, if of the heaven-sent fates
One did not check the other,

Cancel the other's advantage,
My heart would outrun my tongue
In pouring out these fears.
But now it mutters in the dark,
Embittered, no way hoping
To unravel a scheme in time
    From a burning mind.

    (CLYTEMNESTRA *appears in the door of the palace.*)

CLYT. Go in too, you; I speak to you, Cassandra,
Since God in his clemency has put you in this house
To share our holy water, standing with many
    slaves
Beside the altar that protects the house,
Step down from the car there, do not be over-
    proud.
Heracles himself they say was once
Sold, and endured to eat the bread of slavery.
But should such a chance inexorably fall,
There is much advantage in masters who have long
    been rich.
Those who have reaped a crop they never expected
Are in all things hard on their slaves and overstep
    the line.
From us you will have the treatment of tradition.

LEADER OF CHORUS.
You, it is you she has addressed, and clearly.
Caught as you are in these predestined toils
Obey her if you can. But should you disobey . . .

CLYT. If she has more than the gibberish of the swallow,
An unintelligible barbaric speech,
I hope to read her mind, persuade her reason.

LEADER. As things now stand for you, she says the best.
Obey her; leave that car and follow her.

CLYT.
    I have no leisure to waste out here, outside the door.
    Before the hearth in the middle of my house
    The victims stand already, wait the knife.
    You, if you will obey me, waste no time.
    But if you cannot understand my language—
                (*to* CHORUS LEADER)
    You make it plain to her with the brute and voice-
        less hand.
LEADER. The stranger seems to need a clear interpreter.
    She bears herself like a wild beast newly captured.
CLYT. The fact is she is mad, she listens to evil thoughts,
    Who has come here leaving a city newly captured
    Without experience how to bear the bridle
    So as not to waste her strength in foam and blood.
    I will not spend more words to be ignored.
                (*She re-enters the palace.*)
CHORUS. But I, for I pity her, will not be angry.
    Obey, unhappy woman. Leave this car.
    Yield to your fate. Put on the untried yoke.
CASS. Apollo! Apollo!
CHORUS. Why do you cry like this upon Apollo?
    He is not the kind of god that calls for dirges.
CASS. Apollo! Apollo!
CHORUS. Once more her funereal cries invoke the god
    Who has no place at the scene of lamentation.
CASS. Apollo! Apollo!
    God of the Ways! My destroyer!
    Destroyed again—and this time utterly!
CHORUS.
    She seems about to predict her own misfortunes.
    The gift of the god endures, even in a slave's mind.
CASS. Apollo! Apollo!

God of the Ways! My destroyer!
Where? To what house? Where, where have you
   brought me?

CHORUS. To the house of the sons of Atreus. If you do
      not know it,
   I will tell you so. You will not find it false.

CASS. No, no, but to a god-hated, but to an accomplice
   In much kin-killing, murdering nooses,
   Man-shambles, a floor asperged with blood.

CHORUS.
   The stranger seems like a hound with a keen scent,
   Is picking up a trail that leads to murder.

CASS. Clues! I have clues! Look! They are these.
   These wailing, these children, butchery of children;
   Roasted flesh, a father sitting to dinner.

CHORUS. Of your prophetic fame we have heard before
   But in this matter prophets are not required.

CASS. What is she doing? What is she planning?
   What is this new great sorrow?
   Great crime . . . within here . . . planning
   Unendurable to his folk, impossible
   Ever to be cured. For help
      Stands far distant.

CHORUS. This reference I cannot catch. But the children
   I recognized; that refrain is hackneyed.

CASS. Damned, damned, bringing this work to com-
      pletion—
   Your husband who shared your bed
   To bathe him, to cleanse him, and then—
   How shall I tell of the end?
   Soon, very soon, it will fall.
      The end comes hand over hand
      Grasping in greed.

50

CHORUS.
    Not yet do I understand. After her former riddles
    Now I am baffled by these dim pronouncements.
CASS. Ah God, the vision! God, God, the vision!
    A net, is it? Net of Hell!
    But herself is the net; shared bed; shares murder.
    O let the pack ever-hungering after the family
    Howl for the unholy ritual, howl for the victim.
CHORUS.
    What black Spirit is this you call upon the house—
    To raise aloft her cries? Your speech does not
        lighten me.
    Into my heart runs back the blood
    Yellow as when for men by the spear fallen
    The blood ebbs out with the rays of the setting life
        And death strides quickly.
CASS. Quick! Be on your guard! The bull—
    Keep him clear of the cow.
    Caught with a trick, the black horn's point,
    She strikes. He falls; lies in the water.
    Murder; a trick in a bath. I tell what I see.
CHORUS. I would not claim to be expert in oracles
    But these, as I deduce, portend disaster.
    Do men ever get a good answer from oracles?
    No. It is only through disaster
    That their garrulous craft brings home
    The meaning of the prophet's panic.
CASS. And for me also, for me, chance ill-destined!
    My own now I lament, pour into the cup my own.
    Where is this you have brought me in my misery?
    Unless to die as well. What else is meant?
CHORUS. You are mad, mad, carried away by the god,
    Raising the dirge, the tuneless

Tune, for yourself. Like the tawny
Unsatisfied singer from her luckless heart
Lamenting 'Itys, Itys', the nightingale
Lamenting a life luxuriant with grief.

CASS. Oh the lot of the songful nightingale!
The gods enclosed her in a winged body,
Gave her a sweet and tearless passing.
But for me remains the two-edged cutting blade.

CHORUS. From whence these rushing and God-inflicted
Profitless pains?
Why shape with your sinister crying
The piercing hymn—fear-piercing?
How can you know the evil-worded landmarks
On the prophetic path?

CASS. Oh the wedding, the wedding of Paris—death to
his people!
O river Scamander, water drunk by my fathers!
When I was young, alas, upon your beaches
I was brought up and cared for.
But now it is the River of Wailing and the banks of
Hell
That shall hear my prophecy soon.

CHORUS. What is this clear speech, too clear?
A child could understand it.
I am bitten with fangs that draw blood
By the misery of your cries,
Cries harrowing the heart.

CASS. Oh trouble on trouble of a city lost, lost utterly!
My father's sacrifices before the towers,
Much killing of cattle and sheep,
No cure—availed not at all
To prevent the coming of what came to Troy,
And I, my brain on fire, shall soon enter the trap.

CHORUS. This speech accords with the former.
>What god, malicious, over-heavy, persistently
>>pressing,
>Drives you to chant of these lamentable
>Griefs with death their burden?
>But I cannot see the end.
>>(CASSANDRA *now steps down from the car*.)
CASS. The oracle now no longer from behind veils
>Will be peeping forth like a newly-wedded bride;
>But I can feel it like a fresh wind swoop
>And rush in the face of the dawn and, wave-like,
>>wash
>Against the sun a vastly greater grief
>Than this one. I shall speak no more conundrums.
>And bear me witness, pacing me, that I
>Am trailing on the scent of ancient wrongs.
>For this house here a choir never deserts,
>Chanting together ill. For they mean ill,
>And to puff up their arrogance they have drunk
>Men's blood, this band of revellers that haunts the
>>house,
>Hard to be rid of, fiends that attend the family.
>Established in its rooms they hymn their hymn
>Of that original sin, abhor in turn
>The adultery that proved a brother's ruin.
>A miss? Or do my arrows hit the mark?
>Or am I a quack prophet who knocks at doors, a
>>babbler?
>Give me your oath, confess I have the facts,
>The ancient history of this house's crimes.
LEADER. And how could an oath's assurance, however
>finely assured,
>Turn out a remedy? I wonder, though, that you

53

Being brought up overseas, of another tongue,
Should hit on the whole tale as if you had been
    standing by.

CASS. Apollo the prophet set me to prophesy.

LEADER. Was he, although a god, struck by desire?

CASS. Till now I was ashamed to tell that story.

LEADER. Yes. Good fortune keeps us all fastidious.

CASS. He wrestled hard upon me, panting love.

LEADER.
    And did you come, as they do, to child-getting?

CASS. No. I agreed to him. And I cheated him.

LEADER. Were you already possessed by the mystic art?

CASS. Already I was telling the townsmen all their future
    suffering.

LEADER. Then how did you escape the doom of Apollo's
    anger?

CASS. I did not escape. No one ever believed me.

LEADER. Yet to us your words seem worthy of belief.

CASS. Oh misery, misery!
    Again comes on me the terrible labour of true
Prophecy, dizzying prelude; distracts . . .
Do you see these who sit before the house,
Children, like the shapes of dreams?
Children who seem to have been killed by their
    kinsfolk,
Filling their hands with meat, flesh of themselves,
Guts and entrails, handfuls of lament—
Clear what they hold—the same their father tasted.
For this I declare someone is plotting vengeance—
A lion? Lion but coward, that lurks in bed,
Good watchdog truly against the lord's return—
My lord, for I must bear the yoke of serfdom.
Leader of the ships, overturner of Troy,

He does not know what plots the accursed hound
With the licking tongue and the pricked-up ear
 will plan
In the manner of a lurking doom, in an evil hour.
A daring criminal! Female murders male.
What monster could provide her with a title?
An amphisbaena or hag of the sea who dwells
In rocks to ruin sailors—
A raving mother of death who breathes against her
 folk
War to the finish. Listen to her shout of triumph,
Who shirks no horrors, like men in a rout of battle.
And yet she poses as glad at their return.
If you distrust my words, what does it matter?
That which will come will come. You too will soon
 stand here
And admit with pity that I spoke too truly.

LEADER. Thyestes' dinner of his children's meat
I understood and shuddered, and fear grips me
To hear the truth, not framed in parables.
But hearing the rest I am thrown out of my course.

CASS. It is Agamemnon's death I tell you you shall
 witness.

LEADER. Stop! Provoke no evil. Quiet your mouth!

CASS. The god who gives me words is here no healer.

LEADER. Not if this shall be so. But may some chance
 avert it.

CASS.
 You are praying. But others are busy with murder.

LEADER. What man is he promotes this terrible thing?

CASS.
 Indeed you have missed my drift by a wide margin!

LEADER. But I do not understand the assassin's method.

55

CASS. And yet too well I know the speech of Greece!
LEADER. So does Delphi but the replies are hard.
CASS. Ah what a fire it is! It comes upon me.

Apollo, Wolf-Destroyer, pity, pity . . .
It is the two-foot lioness who beds
Beside a wolf, the noble lion away,
It is she will kill me. Brewing a poisoned cup
She will mix my punishment too in the angry
    draught
And boasts, sharpening the dagger for her husband,
To pay back murder for my bringing here.
Why then do I wear these mockeries of myself,
The wand and the prophet's garland round my
    neck?
My hour is coming—but you shall perish first.
Destruction! Scattered thus you give me my
    revenge;
Go and enrich some other woman with ruin.
See: Apollo himself is stripping me
Of my prophetic gear, who has looked on
When in this dress I have been a laughing-stock
To friends and foes alike, and to no purpose;
They called me crazy, like a fortune-teller,
A poor starved beggar-woman—and I bore it.
And now the prophet undoing his prophetess
Has brought me to this final darkness.
Instead of my father's altar the executioner's block
Waits me the victim, red with my hot blood.
But the gods will not ignore me as I die.
One will come after to avenge my death,
A matricide, a murdered father's champion.
Exile and tramp and outlaw he will come back
To gable the family house of fatal crime;

His father's outstretched corpse shall lead him
    home.
Why need I then lament so pitifully?
For now that I have seen the town of Troy
Treated as she was treated, while her captors
Come to their reckoning thus by the gods' verdict,
I will go in and have the courage to die.
Look, these gates are the gates of Death. I greet
    them.
And I pray that I may meet a deft and mortal stroke
So that without a struggle I may close
My eyes and my blood ebb in easy death.

LEADER. Oh woman very unhappy and very wise,
    Your speech was long. But if in sober truth
    You know your fate, why like an ox that the gods
    Drive, do you walk so bravely to the altar?

CASS. There is no escape, strangers. No; not by post-
    ponement.

LEADER. But the last moment has the privilege of hope.

CASS. The day is here. Little should I gain by flight.

LEADER. This patience of yours comes from a brave
    soul.

CASS. A happy man is never paid that compliment.

LEADER. But to die with credit graces a mortal man.

CASS. Oh my father! You and your noble sons!

       (*She approaches the door, then suddenly recoils.*)

LEADER.
    What is it? What is the fear that drives you back?

CASS. Faugh.

LEADER. Why faugh? Or is this some hallucination?

CASS. These walls breathe out a death that drips with
    blood.

LEADER. Not so. It is only the smell of the sacrifice.

CASS. It is like a breath out of a charnel-house.

LEADER. You think our palace burns odd incense then!

CASS. But I will go to lament among the dead
My lot and Agamemnon's. Enough of life!
Strangers,
I am not afraid like a bird afraid of a bush
But witness you my words after my death
When a woman dies in return for me a woman
And a man falls for a man with a wicked wife.
I ask this service, being about to die.

LEADER.
Alas, I pity you for the death you have foretold.

CASS.
One more speech I have; I do not wish to raise
The dirge for my own self. But to the sun I pray
In face of his last light that my avengers
May make my murderers pay for this my death,
Death of a woman slave, an easy victim.

(*She enters the palace.*)

LEADER.
Ah the fortunes of men! When they go well
A shadow sketch would match them, and in ill-
fortune
The dab of a wet sponge destroys the drawing.
It is not myself but the life of man I pity.

CHORUS. Prosperity in all men cries
For more prosperity. Even the owner
Of the finger-pointed-at palace never shuts
His door against her, saying 'Come no more'.
So to our king the blessed gods had granted
To take the town of Priam, and heaven-favoured
He reaches home. But now if for former bloodshed
He must pay blood

58

And dying for the dead shall cause
>Other deaths in atonement
What man could boast he was born
>Secure, who heard this story?

AGAM.

>(*within*) Oh! I am struck a mortal blow—within!

LEADER.

>Silence! Listen. Who calls out, wounded with a
>>mortal stroke?

AGAM.

>Again—the second blow—I am struck again.

LEADER.

>You heard the king cry out. I think the deed is done.
>Let us see if we can concert some sound proposal.

2ND OLD MAN.

>Well, I will tell you my opinion—
>Raise an alarm, summon the folk to the palace.

3RD OLD MAN.

>I say burst in with all speed possible,
>Convict them of the deed while still the sword is
>>wet.

4TH OLD MAN.

>And I am partner to some such suggestion.
>I am for taking some course. No time to dawdle.

5TH OLD MAN.

>The case is plain. This is but the beginning.
>They are going to set up dictatorship in the state.

6TH OLD MAN.

>We are wasting time. The assassins tread to earth
>The decencies of delay and give their hands no sleep.

7TH OLD MAN.

>I do not know what plan I could hit on to propose.
>The man who acts is in the position to plan.

8TH OLD MAN.

> So I think, too, for I am at a loss
> To raise the dead man up again with words.

9TH OLD MAN.

> Then to stretch out our life shall we yield thus
> To the rule of these profaners of the house?

10TH OLD MAN.

> It is not to be endured. To die is better.
> Death is more comfortable than tyranny.

11TH OLD MAN.

> And are we on the evidence of groans
> Going to give oracle that the prince is dead?

12TH OLD MAN.

> We must know the facts for sure and *then* be angry.
> Guesswork is not the same as certain knowledge.

LEADER.

> Then all of you back me and approve this plan—
> To ascertain how it is with Agamemnon.

> > (*The doors of the palace open, revealing the bodies
> > of* AGAMEMNON *and* CASSANDRA. CLY-
> > TEMNESTRA *stands above them.*)

CLYT.

> Much having been said before to fit the moment,
> To say the opposite now will not outface me.
> How else could one serving hate upon the hated,
> Thought to be friends, hang high the nets of doom
> To preclude all leaping out?
> For me I have long been training for this match,
> I tried a fall and won—a victory overdue.
> I stand here where I struck, above my victims;
> So I contrived it—this I will not deny—
> That he could neither fly nor ward off death;
> Inextricable like a net for fishes

I cast about him a vicious wealth of raiment
And struck him twice and with two groans he
    loosed
His limbs beneath him, and upon him fallen
I deal him the third blow to the God beneath the
    earth,
To the safe keeper of the dead a votive gift,
And with that he spits his life out where he lies
And smartly spouting blood he sprays me with
The sombre drizzle of bloody dew and I
Rejoice no less than in God's gift of rain
The crops are glad when the ear of corn gives
    birth.
These things being so, you, elders of Argos,
Rejoice if rejoice you will. Mine is the glory.
And if I could pay this corpse his due libation
I should be right to pour it and more than right;
With so many horrors this man mixed and filled
The bowl—and, coming home, has drained the
    draught himself.

LEADER.

Your speech astonishes us. This brazen boast
Above the man who was your king and husband!

CLYT.

You challenge me as a woman without foresight
But I with unflinching heart to you who know
Speak. And you, whether you will praise or blame,
It makes no matter. Here lies Agamemnon,
My husband, dead, the work of this right hand,
An honest workman. There you have the facts.

CHORUS. Woman, what poisoned
Herb of the earth have you tasted
Or potion of the flowing sea

61

To undertake this killing and the people's curses?
You threw down, you cut off—The people will cast
    you out,
Black abomination to the town.

CLYT. Now your verdict—in my case—is exile
And to have the people's hatred, the public curses,
Though then in no way you opposed this man
Who carelessly, as if it were a head of sheep
Out of the abundance of his fleecy flocks,
Sacrificed his own daughter, to me the dearest
Fruit of travail, charm for the Thracian winds.
He was the one to have banished from this land,
Pay off the pollution. But when you hear what I
Have done, you judge severely. But I warn you—
Threaten me on the understanding that I am ready
For two alternatives—Win by force the right
To rule me, but, if God brings about the contrary,
Late in time you will have to learn self-discipline.

CHORUS. You are high in the thoughts,
You speak extravagant things,
After the soiling murder your crazy heart
Fancies your forehead with a smear of blood.
Unhonoured, unfriended, you must
Pay for a blow with a blow.

CLYT. Listen then to this—the sanction of my oaths:
By the Justice totting up my child's atonement,
By the Avenging Doom and Fiend to whom I
    killed this man,
For me hope walks not in the rooms of fear
So long as my fire is lit upon my hearth
By Aegisthus, loyal to me as he was before.
The man who outraged me lies here,
The darling of each courtesan at Troy,

62

And here with him is the prisoner clairvoyante,
The fortune-teller that he took to bed,
Who shares his bed as once his bench on shipboard,
A loyal mistress. Both have their deserts.
He lies so; and she who like a swan
Sang her last dying lament
Lies his lover, and the sight contributes
An appetiser to my own bed's pleasure.

CHORUS.
Ah would some quick death come not overpainful,
Not overlong on the sickbed,
Establishing in us the ever-
Lasting unending sleep now that our guardian
Has fallen, the kindest of men,
Who suffering much for a woman
By a woman has lost his life.
O Helen, insane, being one
One to have destroyed so many
And many souls under Troy,
Now is your work complete, blossomed not for
    oblivion,
Unfading stain of blood. Here now, if in any
    home,
Is Discord, here is a man's deep-rooted ruin.

CLYT. Do not pray for the portion of death
Weighed down by these things, do not turn
Your anger on Helen as destroyer of men,
One woman destroyer of many
Lives of Greek men,
A hurt that cannot be healed.

CHORUS. O Evil Spirit, falling on the family,
On the two sons of Atreus and using
Two sisters in heart as your tools,

63

A power that bites to the heart—
See on the body
Perched like a raven he gloats
Harshly croaking his hymn.

CLYT. Ah, now you have amended your lips' opinion,
Calling upon this family's three times gorged
Genius—demon who breeds
Blood-hankering lust in the belly:
Before the old sore heals, new pus collects.

CHORUS. It is a great spirit—great—
You tell of, harsh in anger,
A ghastly tale, alas,
Of unsatisfied disaster
Brought by Zeus, by Zeus,
Cause and worker of all.
For without Zeus what comes to pass among us?
Which of these things is outside Providence?
O my king, my king,
How shall I pay you in tears,
Speak my affection in words?
You lie in that spider's web,
In a desecrating death breathe out your life,
Lie ignominiously
Defeated by a crooked death
And the two-edged cleaver's stroke.

CLYT. You say this is *my* work—mine?
Do not cozen yourself that I am Agamemnon's
wife.
Masquerading as the wife
Of the corpse there the old sharp-witted Genius
Of Atreus who gave the cruel banquet
Has paid with a grown man's life
The due for children dead.

CHORUS. That you are not guilty of
        This murder who will attest?
        No, but you may have been abetted
        By some ancestral Spirit of Revenge.
        Wading a millrace of the family's blood
        The black Manslayer forces a forward path
        To make the requital at last
        For the eaten children, the blood-clot cold with time.
            O my king, my king,
            How shall I pay you in tears,
            Speak my affection in words?
            You lie in that spider's web,
            In a desecrating death breathe out your life,
            Lie ignominiously
            Defeated by a crooked death
            And the two-edged cleaver's stroke.
CLYT. Did he not, too, contrive a crooked
        Horror for the house? My child by him,
        Shoot that I raised, much-wept-for Iphigeneia,
        He treated her like this;
        So suffering like this he need not make
        Any great brag in Hell having paid with death
        Dealt by the sword for work of his own beginning.
CHORUS. I am at a loss for thought, I lack
        All nimble counsel as to where
        To turn when the house is falling.
        I fear the house-collapsing crashing
        Blizzard of blood—of which these drops are earnest.
        Now is Destiny sharpening her justice
        On other whetstones for a new infliction.
            O earth, earth, if only you had received me
            Before I saw this man lie here as if in bed
                In a bath lined with silver.

Who will bury him? Who will keen him?
Will you, having killed your own husband,
Dare now to lament him
And after great wickedness make
    Unamending amends to his ghost?
And who above this godlike hero's grave
Pouring praises and tears
    Will grieve with a genuine heart?

CLYT. It is not your business to attend to that.
By my hand he fell low, lies low and dead,
And I shall bury him low down in the earth,
And his household need not weep him
For Iphigeneia his daughter
Tenderly, as is right,
Will meet her father at the rapid ferry of sorrows,
Put her arms round him and kiss him!

CHORUS. Reproach answers reproach,
It is hard to decide,
The catcher is caught, the killer pays for his kill.
But the law abides while Zeus abides enthroned
That the wrongdoer suffers. That is established.
Who could expel from the house the seed of the
    Curse?
The race is soldered in sockets of Doom and
    Vengeance.

CLYT.
In this you say what is right and the will of God.
But for my part I am ready to make a contract
With the Evil Genius of the House of Atreus
To accept what has been till now, hard though it is,
But that for the future he shall leave this house
And wear away some other stock with deaths
Imposed among themselves. Of my possessions

66

A small part will suffice if only I
Can rid these walls of the mad exchange of murder.
(*Enter* Aegisthus, *followed by soldiers.*)
AEG. O welcome light of a justice-dealing day!
From now on I will say that the gods, avenging
 men,
Look down from above on the crimes of earth,
Seeing as I do in woven robes of the Furies
This man lying here—a sight to warm my heart—
Paying for the crooked violence of his father.
For his father Atreus, when he ruled the country,
Because his power was challenged, hounded out
From state and home his own brother Thyestes.
My father—let me be plain—was this Thyestes,
Who later came back home a suppliant,
There, miserable, found so much asylum
As not to die on the spot, stain the ancestral floor.
But to show his hospitality godless Atreus
Gave him an eager if not a loving welcome,
Pretending a day of feasting and rich meats
Served my father with his children's flesh.
The hands and feet, fingers and toes, he hid
At the bottom of the dish. My father sitting apart
Took unknowing the unrecognizable portion
And ate of a dish that has proved, as you see,
 expensive.
But when he knew he had eaten worse than poison
He fell back groaning, vomiting their flesh,
And invoking a hopeless doom on the sons of
 Pelops
Kicked over the table to confirm his curse—
So may the whole race perish!
Result of this—you see this man lie here.

I stitched this murder together; it was my title.
Me the third son he left, an unweaned infant,
To share the bitterness of my father's exile.
But I grew up and Justice brought me back,
I grappled this man while still beyond his door,
Having pieced together the programme of his ruin.
So now would even death be beautiful to me
Having seen Agamemnon in the nets of Justice.

LEADER.

Aegisthus. I cannot respect brutality in distress.
You claim that you deliberately killed this prince
And that you alone planned this pitiful murder.
Be sure that in your turn your head shall not escape
The people's volleyed curses mixed with stones.

AEG. Do you speak so who sit at the lower oar
While those on the upper bench control the ship?
Old as you are, you will find it is a heavy load
To go to school when old to learn the lesson of tact.
For old age, too, gaol and hunger are fine
Instructors in wisdom, second-sighted doctors.
You have eyes. Cannot you see?
Do not kick against the pricks. The blow will hurt
      you.

LEADER. You woman waiting in the house for those who
      return from battle
While you seduce their wives! Was it you devised
The death of a master of armies?

AEG. And these words, too, prepare the way for tears.
Contrast your voice with the voice of Orpheus: he
Led all things after him bewitched with joy, but you
Having stung me with your silly yelps shall be
Led off yourself, to prove more mild when
      mastered.

68

LEADER. Indeed! So you are now to be king of Argos,
    You who, when you had plotted the king's death,
    Did not even dare to do that thing yourself!

AEG. No. For the trick of it was clearly woman's work.
    I was suspect, an enemy of old.
    But now I shall try with Agamemnon's wealth
    To rule the people. Any who is disobedient
    I will harness in a heavy yoke, no tracehorse work
        for him
    Like barley-fed colt, but hateful hunger lodging
    Beside him in the dark will see his temper soften.

LEADER.
    Why with your cowardly soul did you yourself
    Not strike this man but left that work to a woman
    Whose presence pollutes our country and its gods?
    But Orestes—does he somewhere see the light
    That he may come back here by favour of fortune
    And kill this pair and prove the final victor?

AEG. (*Summoning his guards.*)
    Well, if such is your design in deeds and words, you
        will quickly learn—
    Here my friends, here my guards, there is work for
        you at hand.

LEADER.
    Come then, hands on hilts, be each and all of us
        prepared.
    (*The old men and the guards threaten each other.*)

AEG.
    Very well! I too am ready to meet death with
        sword in hand.

LEADER.
    We are glad you speak of dying. We accept your
        words for luck.

CLYT.

No, my dearest, do not so. Add no more to the
train of wrong.

To reap these many present wrongs is harvest
enough of misery.

Enough of misery. Start no more. Our hands are
red.

But do you, and you old men, go home and yield
to fate in time,

In time before you suffer. We have acted as we had
to act.

If only our afflictions now could prove enough, we
should agree—

We who have been so hardly mauled in the heavy
claws of the evil god.

So stands my word, a woman's, if any man thinks
fit to hear.

AEG.

But to think that these should thus pluck the
blooms of an idle tongue

And should throw out words like these, giving the
evil god his chance,

And should miss the path of prudence and insult
their master so!

LEADER.

It is not the Argive way to fawn upon a cowardly
man.

AEG.

Perhaps. But I in later days will take further steps
with you.

LEADER.

Not if the god who rules the family guides Orestes
to his home.

AEG.

Yes. I know that men in exile feed themselves on
barren hopes.

LEADER.

Go on, grow fat defiling justice . . . while you have
your hour.

AEG.

Do not think you will not pay me a price for your
stupidity.

LEADER.

Boast on in your self-assurance, like a cock beside
his hen.

CLYT.

Pay no heed, Aegisthus, to these futile barkings.
You and I,

Masters of this house, from now shall order all
things well.

(*They enter the palace.*)